D0646287

TEEN LIFE™

FREQUENTLY ASKED QUESTIONS ABOUT

# MyPyramid:
## Eating Right

Kara Williams

ROSEN
PUBLISHING®

New York

Published in 2007 by The Rosen Publishing Group, Inc.
29 East 21st Street, New York, NY 10010

First Edition

**Library of Congress Cataloging-in-Publication Data**

Williams, Kara.
Frequently asked questions about mypyramid : eating right /
Kara Williams.
p. cm. — (Faq: teen life)
ISBN-13: 978-1-4042-1974-8
ISBN-10: 1-4042-1974-9
1. Nutrition—Juvenile literature. 2. Food—Juvenile literature.
3. Health—Juvenile literature. I. Title. II. Title: Frequently asked
questions about my pyramid.
RA784.W5544 2006
613.2—dc22

2006033523

*Manufactured in the United States of America*

# Contents

# Introduction

**Y**ou are what you eat. This phrase may be a cliché, but it also happens to be true. What goes into your body determines your physical and emotional health. It affects how you feel physically and how you feel about yourself. Food contains the nutrients and energy your body needs to stay alive. The quality of your life—your health and vitality—depends on the balance of foods you eat every day. Understanding what good nutrition is can help you make better choices about your diet and improve your health.

## A New and Improved Personalized Pyramid

In 1992, the United States Department of Agriculture (USDA) created its food guide pyramid—a simple graphic that outlined the ideal daily balance of different kinds of foods and nutrients that will result in good nutrition and a healthy weight. In 2005, the USDA revamped the pyramid design, based on the *Dietary Guidelines for Americans,* which are updated every five years by the USDA and the U.S. Department of Health and Human Services (HHS).

Realizing that one size does not fit all and that the amount of ideal food intake differs depending on a person's

In April 2006, the University of California, Berkeley, opened the nation's first college campus organic salad bar. The university plans to extend this service to all of its dining halls by spring 2007.

age, gender, and activity level, the government changed the name of the food pyramid to MyPyramid and unveiled a Web site, www.MyPyramid.gov, that customizes a healthy eating and exercise plan that's just right for you. The new MyPyramid interactive food guidance system—which differs greatly from the 1992 food pyramid—is designed to help Americans live longer, better, and healthier lives. In creating the interactive MyPyramid plan, the USDA is committed to combating the obesity epidemic in the United States.

# one

## WHAT IS MYPYRAMID?

It's been in the news for years: Americans are getting bigger. And the epidemic is not limited to adults. In 2002, approximately 30 percent of U.S. children ages six to eleven were overweight and 15 percent were obese. Of adolescents ages twelve to nineteen, 30 percent were overweight and 16 percent were obese, according to the American Obesity Association, and those numbers are growing every year.

Overweight children tend to become overweight adults. More than 100 million Americans are now obese or overweight. It is clear that the more overweight you are, the more you are at risk for diabetes, cancer, and heart disease—all life-threatening conditions.

Given the increasing numbers of overweight Americans, it makes sense that the USDA would release an easy-to-follow MyPyramid plan that outlines healthy

Fast food contains trans fats, which contribute to heart disease. In response, New York City's health department announced a proposal in September 2006 to ban cooking oils and other ingredients with trans fats in the city's restaurants.

food recommendations *and* daily exercise. However, MyPyramid is just a guide to good nutrition and healthy living. It can make recommendations, but it cannot force people to follow them. How you use the nutrition information provided by MyPyramid is up to you.

## The First Step to Good Health

If taking note of what you're putting in your mouth is new to you, just take it slow and make it simple. In following the

Obesity is not only a problem in the United States. A study reports that in the United Kingdom one out of three adults and one out of five children will be obese by 2010.

MyPyramid guidelines, you do not have to carry a calculator around with you to count every single calorie. You don't need to keep in your pocket lists of ingredients and nutrients to analyze everything you eat. You just need to know a few things about nutrition—what is good for you and what is not so good— to help you make smart decisions about what to eat and what not to eat. You'll quickly get into the habit of thinking about what you choose to eat and choosing foods that will help you stay healthy. Before long, proper daily nutrition will be second nature to you.

# Nutrition

The term "nutrition" refers to all the processes related to the eating and digesting of food and the breaking down of food and its nutrients into energy. It also refers to the processes related to the growth, repair, and maintenance of the living cells of the human body, processes that are fueled by the energy and nutrients provided by the food we eat.

In poor countries, millions of people suffer from malnutrition. They do not have enough food to eat, and the food they eat is often of poor quality. Surprisingly, in rich countries like the United States, malnutrition is also a problem. Some people in the United States still do not have enough to eat, despite the wealth of our nation. And millions of people eat too much food that is not nutritious, which makes them overweight or obese. Putting into practice the basic principles of nutrition can help you create a healthy diet, reach and maintain a healthy weight, and enjoy a long and healthy life.

# two

## HOW ARE ENERGY AND CALORIES RELATED?

Your body is a complex machine that is working all the time, around the clock. At every moment of the day, your heart is beating. Your lungs are taking in air. Blood is circulating through your veins and arteries (the tubelike vessels that carry blood to and from your heart throughout the body). Your bones, muscles, and skin are growing, repairing bits of themselves, and generally keeping themselves in good condition.

Even when you are not doing anything active (when you are sleeping, for example, or lying on the couch and watching television), your body's machinery is working ceaselessly on the inside. This constant work requires energy even if you are lying down or sitting still. You are not always at rest, however. Throughout the day you use your body to perform physical activities. You stand up. You walk and run. You sit down. You eat. You play. This, too, requires

Poor eating habits can negatively affect your academic performance if your diet does not adequately provide the energy you need to remain alert and focus on studying.

energy. Your body gets the energy it needs to function properly from food.

## Energy Comes from Food

The amount of energy contained in food and the amount of energy your body burns is measured in calories. A calorie is a unit of measure that indicates how much energy a specific food will provide. When we say a particular food has a certain number of calories, what we mean is that the food will provide a certain amount of energy. And when we say a particular activity

# Myths and Facts

## About Diet and Nutrition

**Myth**

**I'm skinny. I don't have to worry about any dietary guidelines.** Fact ➠ If you care about your health, about being underweight or overweight, about getting a serious disease, or about dying too young, then you must also care about what you eat. Learning about nutrition is the first step in creating a better diet and a healthier lifestyle. The next step is putting that knowledge into practice. Think about what you eat: about the calories you consume; the energy you burn through exercise; and the amount, variety, and nutritional value of the food in your daily diet. Use MyPyramid as a guide for choosing the widest variety and most nutritious of foods and as a tool in achieving a healthy balance among the main food groups. "Skinny" people who do not eat healthily and do not exercise may actually be "fat." They may have a high percentage of body fat, which may lead to diabetes, cancer, and heart disease.

**Maintaining a healthy diet means I can't eat anything I love—pizza, cake, or ice cream.** Fact ●➤

Adhering to your MyPyramid recommendations doesn't mean you have to cut every treat out of your diet. Consider some lower-fat, lower-calorie versions of foods you love: ask for half the cheese on your pizza slice, and choose mushrooms and onions rather than pepperoni. Next time you make a dessert for a special occasion, try angel food cake with strawberries instead of rich chocolate cake with frosting. Order low-fat frozen yogurt instead of high-fat ice cream. The small changes you make can yield huge results when it comes to your health. (And don't forget those discretionary calories for instances when you just can't say no to a bowl of mint chocolate-chip ice cream.)

**I'm a vegetarian and I work out a lot. There's no way I can get in the amount of daily protein that MyPyramid recommends for me.** Fact ●➤

There are several vegetarian protein sources that can help you reach your "meat and beans" daily recommendations—without having to snack on nuts all day. First, review the portion sizes and ounce equivalents of the vegetarian options—you might think you need more food than you do. A bean burger patty or one cup of lentil soup is the same as two one-ounce equivalents. Then experiment with different foods: for example, falafel pitas, tofu and tempeh stir-fries, and hummus dips. If you are an ovo-vegetarian, a person who eats eggs as his or her sole source of animal protein, then stock up on eggs for delicious veggie omelets for breakfast or hard-boiled eggs as snacks.

**If I want to lose weight, I shouldn't eat nuts.**

Fact ➡ Nuts have gotten a bad rap as a food that is high in fat and calories. Actually, a half ounce of almonds (twelve pieces is one serving) has fewer calories than three ounces of cooked chicken breast (also one serving). Granted, nuts are higher in fat than some other protein sources, but most types of nuts are actually an excellent source of healthy, unsaturated fats. (It's saturated fat that can raise the level of LDL cholesterol, "bad" cholesterol, in your blood.) A small handful of almonds, cashews, walnuts or pecans is a great protein-filled snack that contains fiber, vitamin E, and important minerals such as magnesium, zinc, and iron.

**I can eat more low-fat or nonfat foods because they are low in calories.** Fact ➡ Read food labels! A low-fat or nonfat food *can* be lower in calories than the full-fat version of the same product. But often, low-fat or nonfat versions of snack foods contain just as many calories as their full-fat counterparts because of the sugar, flour, or starches added to improve flavor.

(like running for thirty minutes) burns a certain number of calories, what we mean is that the activity requires a certain amount of energy.

## Calories Measure Energy

Calories are a measure of quantity. They measure how much energy is found in the food you eat, as well as how much energy your body uses to keep running smoothly and performing physical and mental activities. According to the Food and Drug Administration (FDA), the typical American needs about 2,000 calories each day, but caloric requirements vary from one person to another. Most people need an amount somewhere between 1,600 and 2,800 calories. Men generally require more calories than women do. Because they are growing—a process that requires larger amounts of energy—children and teenagers require more calories than adults. Most people need fewer calories per day as they get older. Men and women with active lifestyles need more calories than sedentary (nonactive) people who do not burn as much energy through exercise or an otherwise busy daily routine.

Just as important as the quantity of energy we get from food, however, is the quality of that energy. We measure the quality of the energy our food provides by taking into account something else provided by that food—nutrients.

# three

# WHAT ARE NUTRIENTS?

To a greater degree than at any other time in human history, twenty-first-century North Americans have access to an almost infinite variety of diverse foods. Yet all of the thousands of foods available to us in any supermarket today are still made up of only three main nutrients, known as macronutrients: carbohydrates, proteins, and fats. Carbohydrates, proteins, and fats each provide different amounts of energy. One gram of carbohydrate has about four calories of energy, and a gram of protein also provides four calories of energy. Fat provides the most energy per gram, with nine calories.

## Carbohydrates

Digestion breaks down carbohydrates into sugars, starches (which are sugar molecules bonded together), and fiber. Sugars and starches provide your body with

Including fresh fruit such as apples, which are high in fiber, on your grocery shopping list can help you make good eating choices when you feel like snacking.

energy. Any energy you do not use gets stored in your body as fat. Fiber is coarse plant matter that cannot be digested. **Fresh fruits and vegetables, whole-grain cereals, nuts, peas, and beans are all high in fiber.** Even though fiber is not a nutrient, it is very important to your body's health. Fiber, which can only be found in plant foods, aids digestion and can help lower cholesterol. Evidence suggests that a high-fiber diet may lower the risk of some types of cancer. It also helps prevent diseases such as diabetes, heart disease, and an inflammation of the intestine called diverticulitis.

There are two kinds of carbohydrates: simple carbs and complex carbs. Simple carbs are those that are broken down into glucose quickly. Glucose is one of the simplest kinds of sugar molecules and is the body's main source of fuel. The closer something is to glucose, as simple carbs are, the more quickly it is digested and used as fuel. Simple carbs provide an immediate but short-lived burst of energy. They often leave you feeling less energetic than before eating them. Simple carbs include fruit juice, certain fruits, and highly refined food products like white flour, white rice, sugar, breakfast cereals, white bread, white flour pasta, and candy.

More complex, unrefined, unprocessed carbohydrate foods such as whole fresh fruits, fresh vegetables, brown rice, whole wheat, and bran have more indigestible fiber in them. This means they are broken down into glucose more slowly. Because they release sugar into your bloodstream slowly and steadily, they give you sustained energy over a longer time. In addition, complex carbs usually contain more vitamins and minerals than simple and refined carbs, which are so highly processed that they have lost much of their nutritional value.

## Proteins

Proteins are found in every cell of your body. Proteins are made of amino acids, sometimes called the building blocks of life. Your body uses twenty different amino acids. They can be combined, like the ingredients in a recipe, to make the 10,000 or so different proteins of which your body is made. Your body creates eleven of the amino acids it needs to stay in good shape. These are

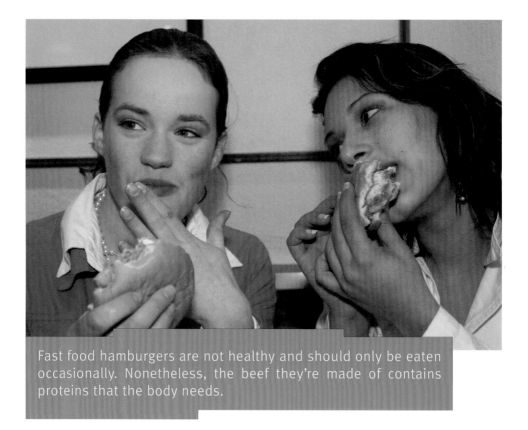

Fast food hamburgers are not healthy and should only be eaten occasionally. Nonetheless, the beef they're made of contains proteins that the body needs.

known as the nonessential amino acids. The other—the essential amino acids—must come from the protein in foods. A little protein goes a long way, however: You need only about one gram of protein for every kilogram of your body weight (1 kg is about 2.2 pounds), and growing teenagers who are involved in sports may need twice that amount. On average, Americans eat about twice as much as they need.

Proteins come from either animal foods (meat, fish, eggs, and dairy products) or from plant foods (cereals, beans, and nuts). Plant foods do not always have all the essential amino acids your body needs to make the various proteins that build up, maintain, and replace the cell tissues in your body. That is why it is important to eat a variety of vegetables, fruits, and cereals that will provide you with all the amino acids your body needs. Protein from animal sources has a more complete range of amino acid ingredients than do plant foods (with the exception of soy and quinoa, which contain all of the essential amino acids). But animal protein foods, like meat, fish, and dairy products, have something that most fruits and vegetables do not have much of—fats.

## Fats

Though we tend to think of fats as harmful, they are just as important to the smooth functioning of your body as are carbohydrates and protein. Fats have more than twice as much concentrated energy as either carbohydrates or protein: nine calories per gram, compared with just four calories per gram of protein and four calories per gram of carbohydrates. In addition, fats help transport and absorb other vitamins in your body.

The amount of fat in your diet is not as important as the type of fat that is found in the foods you eat. Some kinds of fats are better for your health than others. The three main kinds of food fats are saturated fats, unsaturated fats, and trans fats. As we will see below, unsaturated fats are far better for you than either saturated or trans fats.

Saturated fats are mainly animal fats found in meat and dairy products. Some vegetable oils, such as coconut and palm oils, also contain high levels of saturated fats. Unsaturated fats are found mainly in vegetable oils, such as corn, sunflower, soybean,

and olive oils. Trans fats are human-made fats. They are produced when hydrogen is pumped through vegetable oil in order
to change it from a liquid into a solid. This process, called hydrogenation, turns liquid vegetable oil into a solid fat product such
as margarine. Trans fats are listed as hydrogenated or partially
hydrogenated vegetable oil on the nutrition labels of packaged
foods. The food industry uses cooking oils with a lot of trans fats
in them to make cookies, cakes, snack foods, and fast foods.

The quality of these different kinds of fats is related to their
effect on the cholesterol in your body. Like fats, cholesterol has
a bad reputation, though it plays an important role in keeping
the body healthy by coating nerve endings and producing hormones. Cholesterol is a substance in body fluids used to keep
cell walls healthy and to help build cell tissues. The liver makes
cholesterol, which then gets transported in the bloodstream
throughout the body by lipoproteins.

Low-density lipoproteins (LDLs) transport cholesterol away
from the liver. If there is too much LDL cholesterol in the bloodstream, the cholesterol gets deposited on the walls of your body's
arteries. Those cholesterol deposits narrow the arteries, like
grease clogging a drainpipe. Narrowed arteries reduce the flow
of blood to your heart. When that happens, your heart does not
get enough nutrients and oxygen, which can lead to serious
heart disease problems. This is why LDL cholesterol is often
called "bad" cholesterol.

High-density lipoproteins (HDLs) carry unused cholesterol
back from the blood to the liver, which gets rid of it. HDL cholesterol is less likely to be deposited on the walls of arteries. So,

# THE CORONARY ARTERIES

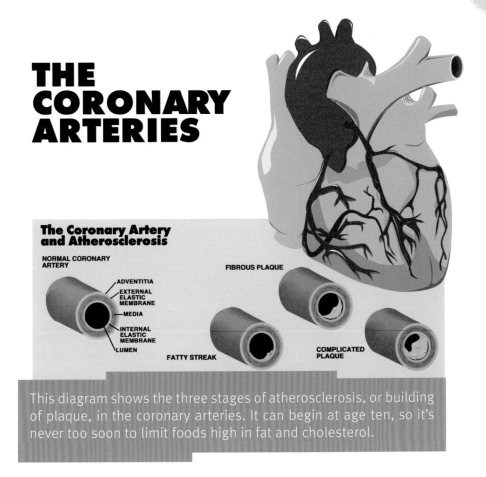

**The Coronary Artery and Atherosclerosis**

NORMAL CORONARY ARTERY

ADVENTITIA

EXTERNAL ELASTIC MEMBRANE

MEDIA

INTERNAL ELASTIC MEMBRANE

LUMEN

FATTY STREAK

FIBROUS PLAQUE

COMPLICATED PLAQUE

This diagram shows the three stages of atherosclerosis, or building of plaque, in the coronary arteries. It can begin at age ten, so it's never too soon to limit foods high in fat and cholesterol.

HDLs keep your arteries clean, thereby reducing the risk of heart disease. This is why HDL cholesterol is often referred to as "good" cholesterol.

What does all this have to do with fats? Unsaturated fats tend to raise the level of good HDL cholesterol and lower the level of bad LDL cholesterol in your blood. Saturated fats tend to raise the level of both types of cholesterol in your blood, both the good HDL and the bad LDL. Trans fats tend to raise the level of bad LDL cholesterol but lower the level of good HDL cholesterol in your blood. So, unsaturated fats actually help to keep your arteries clear. Trans fats and saturated fats can clog up your arteries with cholesterol, which can lead to serious heart disease. That is why unsaturated fats are better for you than saturated fats or trans fats.

Saturated and unsaturated fats are found together in all food fats, but in different proportions. Butter, cheese, and milk, for example, contain mostly saturated fat. Eggs contain mostly unsaturated fats. Most vegetable oils have a lot of unsaturated fats and less saturated fats.

## Vitamins and Minerals

There are two other nutrients in food: vitamins and minerals. These are known as micronutrients. Vitamins are natural substances that are found in both plants and animals. Minerals are substances that originate in rocks and metal ores. Plants obtain minerals from the soil in which they grow, and animals, including humans, absorb these nutrients when they eat plants. Most vitamins and minerals have to come from food because your body cannot make them by itself. Unlike fats, protein, and carbohydrates, vitamins and minerals do not provide energy. Instead, they help regulate the body's processes. Compared with the amount of carbohydrates, protein, and fat your body requires, it needs only tiny amounts of each vitamin and mineral to operate properly.

Different vitamins benefit different parts of your body. Without enough of them—or with too much of them sometimes—your body will not work properly. Vitamin C, for example, helps fight infections and keeps your bones, gums, and teeth healthy.

There's a wide variety of fruits to pick from to get vitamin C. Using MyPyramid can help you decide which ones to eat and determine the proper portion sizes.

Citrus fruits, green peppers, and other fresh fruits and vegetables are the best sources of vitamin C. Vitamin A, also called retinol, plays an important role in vision, bone growth, infection fighting, and regulation of the immune system. Liver, whole milk, eggs, and butter are high in vitamin A. Carrots, cantaloupe, broccoli, and some other fruits and vegetables contain beta-carotene, which the body can convert into vitamin A. Vitamin D helps your body's bones stay strong.

Minerals are inorganic (not living) substances that your body needs to perform many different functions. Calcium, found

Like brushing and flossing, getting enough calcium is important to your dental health. Drinking milk, which is calcium-rich, is a simple way to keep your teeth strong.

mostly in your bones and teeth, is the most abundant mineral in your body. Other minerals crucial to our physical health include phosphorus, sodium, potassium, zinc, iron, chlorine, and magnesium. Small amounts of other minerals, such as copper, cobalt, and iodine, are also present in the human body. These trace minerals are found in much smaller amounts, but they, too, are absolutely essential for the body to function properly.

Like vitamins, specific minerals have specific roles to play in the human body. As we have already learned, calcium is the mineral present in our bodies that builds bones and teeth. To avoid bone loss or weakening, we need to keep our calcium levels adequate by eating foods rich in calcium, such as milk, cheese, yogurt, spinach, and broccoli. Research shows that dietary calcium (rather than calcium taken in supplements, such as vitamin pills) may aid in weight loss because it contributes to increased fat burning rather than fat storage, according to Michael B. Zemel's 2004 article in the *American Journal of Clinical Nutrition.* Iron is mainly used by red blood cells to carry oxygen throughout the body as part of the respiratory cycle. An iron deficiency causes a condition called anemia, in which the number of red blood cells decreases and the body gets less oxygen than it needs, resulting in very low energy. Food such as beef, chicken, tuna, egg yolks, green leafy vegetables, and iron-fortified cereals are excellent natural sources of iron.

# chapter four

## WHAT ARE DIGESTION AND METABOLISM?

Your body derives the energy and nutrients it needs from food by a process called digestion. Nature mixes nutrients and energy to make whole foods, such as fruits, vegetables, and grains. Humans might process these basic foods to create more elaborate products like pasta, bread, soup, vegetable spread, pizza, or cookies. The digestion process uses these nutrients by breaking down the food into its most basic units. This begins happening when you chew food, and it continues in your stomach and intestines. The bloodstream then carries the nutrients to all the cells in your body. Simply put, digestion is the conversion of food into the nutrients and energy that your body needs to stay alive.

## Digestion, Broken Down

Here's how it works: Food goes into your mouth. Your teeth chew the food up into a mush, mixed with saliva.

The digestive system consists of the gastrointestinal tract, which includes the esophagus, stomach, and intestines, and accessory organs, such as the liver, gallbladder, and pancreas.

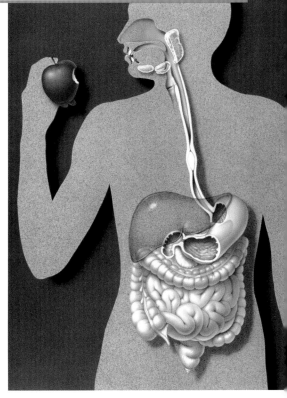

This watery mush is pushed down your esophagus into your stomach. Your stomach walls churn the food up. **Acidic stomach juices break the mush into even smaller bits. The food mush then gets pushed out of your stomach into your small intestine.**

After reaching the small intestine, the mush is further broken down into carbohydrates, proteins, and fats—the three macronutrients. Each macronutrient is further broken down into its smallest parts. So carbohydrates are converted into sugars, proteins into amino acids, and fats into saturated or unsaturated fatty acids. These tiny particles of sugars, amino acids, and fatty acids now pass through the walls of your small intestine into your bloodstream. The sugars and amino acids are absorbed in your blood. Fats are not absorbed, however. Instead, they remain suspended in your blood in tiny droplets called lipoproteins.

Having reached the bloodstream, the nutrient particles are then carried to every part of your body. Their effect is to provide the body with immediate energy and store leftover energy as fat. Equally important, the nutrients keep your body growing and in a state of good health.

Anything in the food mush that cannot be digested—fiber, undigested bits of food, bacteria—is waste and does not enter your bloodstream from the small intestine. Instead, the waste travels into the large intestine. It stays there as solid feces until it is expelled out of your body through the anus.

# Metabolism and the Energy Balance

Food provides the energy your body needs to keep working. Your body burns the energy it gets from the food you eat. You need to eat food regularly to replace the energy the body burns. How much energy you take in from food should be about the same amount of energy your body burns. If you take in more calories than you burn, you'll gain weight.

## Burning Calories at Rest

Your metabolism is the rate at which your body burns energy (calories) in order to keep all the cells and functions of your body working properly. Your basal metabolic rate (BMR) is the number of calories your body burns at rest (without doing physical activities). On average, adults need about 1,500 calories every day just to maintain their BMR. Growing adolescents, from ages fourteen to eighteen, need 45 calories per kilogram, which is

Skateboarding is great exercise and burns 340 calories per hour. However, it would take about an hour and half of ramp time to burn off the calories of a large milkshake!

much more, and may equate to about 2,000 calories each day for girls and about 2,500 calories each day for boys. How much more energy you burn depends on your age, your weight, what physical activities you do, and whether you are a girl, boy, man, or woman.

In order to maintain a healthy weight, the amount of calories you take in through food should be about the same as the amount of calories your body needs for basal metabolism and to perform physical activities. Basal metabolism is the energy required for cell activity, circulation, and breathing by a person at rest. **The more physical activities you do, such as exercise or sports, the** more food energy (calories) you need to take in.

## Balancing What Comes in with What Goes Out

This is known as the energy balance. The energy you take in (as food) should balance the energy being spent on basal metabolism and physical activities. If you eat 2,500 calories of food a day, your body should burn about 2,500 calories a day. If you eat a lot and take in more calories than you burn, the unused energy will be stored in the body as fat. You will gain weight. If you take in fewer calories than you burn, your body will take the extra energy it needs from the fat you have stored in your body. As your body burns up more of this stored fat, you will lose weight.

This simple formula expresses the relationship between calories, metabolism, and weight change:

Teenage boys have high calorie needs, from 2,800 to 4,000 calories a day. However, many still consume more calories than their bodies burn, leading to obesity and difficulty with everyday activities.

## Calories in (what you eat) balanced against calories out (what your body burns) = Weight change

If you take in 2,500 calories a day and burn only 2,000 calories a day, you are eating more than your body is burning, and you will gain weight. If you take in 2,000 calories a day and burn 2,500 calories a day, your body is burning more energy than is provided by the food you are eating, and you will lose weight. If you take in about 2,000 calories a day and burn about 2,000 calories in a day, you're eating just enough food to

# 10 FACTS ABOUT
## FOOD AND NUTRITION

**1** Approximately 30 percent of children ages six to eleven are overweight and 15 percent are obese. Of adolescents ages twelve to nineteen, 30 percent are overweight and 16 percent are obese.

**2** Excess weight leads to at least 300,000 deaths per year in the United States and costs more than $70 billion each year in medical costs. Obesity now accounts for more deaths; serious, long-lasting illnesses; and a poorer quality of life than either smoking or alcohol dependency.

**3** All potatoes are not created equal: A medium serving of french fries from a fast-food restaurant contains 350 calories and 16 grams of fat. A medium-sized baked potato contains 132 calories and 0 grams of fat.

**4** Not used to eating whole grains? Experiment by substituting whole wheat or oat flour for up to half of the flour in pancake, waffle, muffin or other flour-based recipes. (The recipes may need a bit more baking soda or baking powder.)

**5** Certain kinds of fish, such as salmon, trout, and herring, are excellent sources of protein and contain omega-3 fatty acids, which may help fight heart disease.

**6** All fruits are not created equal. A medium-size apple contains 81 calories and 4 grams of dietary fiber. Eight ounces of apple juice contains 123 calories and 0 grams of dietary fiber. Diets rich in fiber may reduce the risk of coronary heart disease.

**7** There are plenty of protein sources for vegetarians: beans, nuts, nut butters, peas, and soy products, such as tofu, tempeh, and veggie burgers. Plus eggs for ovo-vegetarians.

**8** All cereals are not created equal. A cup and a half of corn flakes contains 153 calories. A cup and a half of frosted flakes contains 237 calories, mostly because of the sugar coating.

**9** You can enjoy splurges and maintain a healthy diet. MyPyramid.gov recommends discretionary calories for each user per day, to be used on "extras" like sauces, salad dressings, or sweeteners—or the occasional slice of chocolate cake!

**10** Saturated fats, trans fats, and cholesterol tend to raise "bad" (LDL) cholesterol levels in the blood, which in turn increases the risk for heart disease. To lower your risk for heart disease, cut back on foods containing saturated fats, trans fats, and cholesterol.

Dr. Gillian McKeith, a British nutritionist, signs copies of her best-selling book, *You Are What You Eat*, in London on March 24, 2005. This popular book has been translated into several languages.

meet your body's energy needs, and your weight will stay about the same.

It is almost impossible to achieve an exact balance between the calories you take in and those you burn on any

given day. By keeping this formula in mind, however, you can come close to the proper energy balance and maintain a steady healthy weight over time. To check on how well you are achieving a good energy balance and controlling your weight, you can use a formula called the body mass index.

## The Body Mass Index

The body mass index (BMI) is a formula used to find out if you are underweight, overweight, or about the right weight. A BMI in the range of nineteen to twenty-five is considered a healthy weight. Anything under nineteen is considered underweight, while a reading over twenty-five indicates that a person is overweight. A BMI of thirty or more indicates obesity, a condition that is characterized by excessive body fat.

To determine your body mass index, use the following formula:

1. Divide your weight in pounds by your height in inches.
2. Divide that answer by your height in inches.
3. Multiply that answer by 703.

Let's take, for example, a person who weighs 150 pounds and is 5 feet 6 inches (or 66 inches) tall.

1. Divide weight in pounds (150) by height in inches (66) = 2.27
2. Divide that answer (2.27) by height in inches (66) = 0.034
3. Multiply that answer (0.034) by 703 = 23.9

This person's BMI—twenty-four—is within the normal range of nineteen to twenty-five, so he or she is at a healthy weight. Now use your own weight and height to calculate your BMI. Follow steps one through three as shown in the previous example.

## Your Daily Calorie Requirements

Want a simple, approximate way to find out how many calories a day you need? Multiply your weight in kilograms by twenty-nine if you are not very active (that is, if you do less than thirty minutes of moderate physical exercise every day in addition to your usual daily activities) or by thirty-three if you are very active (if you do moderate physical exercise for more than one hour daily). If you are moderately active, choose a number somewhere in between the two extremes. To convert pounds to kilograms, multiply your weight in pounds by 0.454 (or divide your weight in pounds by 2.2).

Let's say you weigh 110 pounds. That is 50 kilograms (110 x .454 = 50). Let's say you are moderately active, so we will multiply 50 x 31. That is 1,550; so your body needs about 1,550 calories every day to fuel its processes and provide you with the energy you need for your moderate activity. If you are 110 pounds and

# MyPyramid.gov
## STEPS TO A HEALTHIER YOU

The MyPyramid symbol replaced the original food guide pyramid in April 2005. Since then, it has appeared on food packages across the country to promote healthier eating.

very active, multiply 50 by 33. You will need 1,650 calories each day. The Web site www.MyPyramid.gov can help you estimate the number of calories per day you will need for your activity level, age, and gender in the box called My Pyramid Plan.

# five

# WHAT SHOULD I KNOW ABOUT DIETARY GUIDELINES?

Every five years, the U.S. Department of Agriculture (USDA) and the Department of Health and Human Services (HHS) release *Dietary Guidelines for Americans*, science-based advice to promote health and to reduce the risk for major chronic diseases through diet and physical activity. From the 2005 federal nutrition policy came MyPyramid, an educational tool designed to help consumers make healthier food and physical activity choices that are consistent with the guidelines.

Unlike its 1992 food guide pyramid predecessor, MyPyramid is all about customization. At www.MyPyramid.gov, anyone can enter his or her age, gender, and activity level to find out the number of recommended calories needed daily to maintain a healthy weight. The Web site also tells you what and how much of each food you should eat from the different food groups to obtain the proper balance of nutrients you need without taking in too much unhealthy fat, cholesterol, and sugar.

## The MyPyramid Symbol

At first glance, the 2005 MyPyramid symbol may be confusing. Critics have pointed out that unlike the 1992 food pyramid with its diminishing stacks of grains, fruits, vegetables, protein, sweets, and fats, there are no foods pictured!

The USDA explains that one symbol cannot carry all the nutrition guidance and that the new, colorful symbol was designed to be simple, reminding consumers to make healthy food and physical activity choices and be physically active every day.

Here's how the symbol breaks down and what each part represents:

**Activity.** The steps and the person climbing them stand for the significance of performing physical activity every day.

**Moderation.** The narrowing of each food group from bottom to top represents eating foods in moderation. The wide base stands for foods with little or no solid fats or added sugars. These foods should be chosen more frequently. The narrow top area stands for foods that contain more added sugars and solid fats.

**Personalization.** The person on the steps, the slogan "Steps to a Healthier You," and the Web site name MyPyramid.gov represent that every day you can find the types and amounts of food that are right for you to eat at MyPyramid.gov.

**Proportionality.** The different widths of the food group bands show proportionality. The varying widths present how much food you can choose from each group, but they are meant as a general guide, not as exact proportions.

**Variety.** The six color bands symbolize the five food groups and oils of MyPyramid and indicate that food from all the groups are necessary daily for healthy living.

# MyPyramid's Messages For Healthy Living

The basic message of the 2005 Dietary Guidelines for Americans and MyPyramid is to eat well and be active to live longer. Its general recommendations are:

- Eat a variety of foods to get the energy, protein, vitamins, minerals, and fiber you need for good health.
- Balance the food you eat with physical activity—thirty to sixty minutes every day. Maintain or improve your weight to reduce your chances of having high blood pressure, heart disease, a stroke, certain cancers, and the most common kind of diabetes.
- Choose a diet with plenty of whole grain products, vegetables, and fruits, which provide needed vitamins, minerals, fiber, and complex carbohydrates, and can help you lower your intake of fat.

➡️ Choose a diet made up of mostly lean protein sources. Vary those sources to include less meat and more fish, beans, peas, nuts, and seeds.

➡️ Choose a diet moderate in sugars. A diet with lots of sugars has too many calories and too few nutrients for most people and can contribute to tooth decay.

➡️ Choose a diet that limits the intake of saturated and trans fats, which can increase your "bad" blood cholesterol, leading to clogged arteries.

➡️ Choose a diet moderate in salt to help reduce your risk of high blood pressure.

## MyPyramid's Food Recommendations

Plug your age, gender, and activity level into MyPyramid.gov, and you'll learn your daily recommended number of calories and what you should eat from the five food groups. It also gives you an allowance for oils and "discretionary calories," which include solid fats, sugars, and other higher-calorie treats.

Recommended amounts are reported in "ounce equivalents." For example, if your MyPyramid plan suggests you take in six ounces of grains daily (with at least half of them coming from whole grain sources), you might consume one cup of corn flakes (1 ounce), two slices of whole grain bread (2 ounce equivalents), five whole wheat crackers (1 ounce), and 1 cup of spaghetti (2 ounce equivalents).

The site translates how many ounce equivalents there are in many grain sources, such as a bag of microwave popcorn (four),

Waffles and bacon may be delicious to wake up to, but they lack the whole grains found in healthful cereals and the nutrients found in fresh fruit, which are just as satisfying to eat.

a large tortilla (four), and a large muffin (three), as well as ounce equivalents for dozens of items in the other food groups.

Here's the division of categories of the five food groups and a description of the healthy oils and discretionary calories.

## Grains

The orange band is the widest band on the MyPyramid symbol and represents the grains group. This group includes bread, rice, pasta, and cereal. Grains are divided into whole grains (foods that contain the whole grain kernel, such as whole wheat bread,

# Ten Great Questions to Ask About Eating Right

**1** Am I eating the recommended amount of calories for my age, gender, and activity level? If it's too much or too little, what steps can I take to make my calorie intake more appropriate?

**2** Am I eating the recommended amount of grains? Do I know the difference between a whole grain and a refined grain?

**3** Am I eating the recommended portions of vegetables? What sorts of new vegetables can I try this week?

**4** Am I eating the recommended amount of fruits? How much fruit juice do I drink every day?

**5** Am I eating the recommended amount of milk? Is the yogurt, cheese, and milk I consume low fat or fat free?

**6** Am I eating the recommended amount of meat and beans? Do I vary my protein sources enough?

**7** How much oil am I allowed each day? Do I typically consume healthy oils?

**8** How many discretionary calories (extra solid fats and sugars) am I allowed each day?

**9** Am I getting in the recommended thirty to sixty minutes of moderate to vigorous physical activity every day?

**10** Is there anyone else I know who might benefit from dietary guidance?

brown rice, and oatmeal) and refined grains (foods such as white bread, rice, and flour) that have been milled, which is a process that removes the bran and germ). At least half of your daily grain servings should be whole grains. All grains are excellent sources of carbohydrates.

## Vegetables

The next widest food group band on the pyramid, the green band, is the vegetable group. Vegetables can be raw, cooked, fresh, frozen, canned, or dried (also called dehydrated). One hundred percent vegetable juice is included in this group, too. Veggies are divided into five subgroups: dark green, orange, dried beans and peas, starchy, and other. You should try to eat many different kinds of vegetables so that you get the widest possible variety of vitamins and minerals. Also, potatoes may be listed in the vegetable group, but french fries—which are loaded with trans fats—are not included. Eat your potatoes baked, mashed, or boiled (and limit the amount of butter and sour cream that you add to them).

## Milk

The milk, yogurt, and cheese band, the blue band, is about as large as the vegetable band. Dairy foods such as milk, yogurt, and cheese provide your body with calcium, important for the development and strengthening of bones. All fluid milk products and most foods made from milk are regarded as being part of this food group. Foods made from milk that retain their calcium content are part of the group, while foods made from milk that have little to no calcium, such as cream cheese, cream, and butter, are not. Most milk group choices should be fat free or low fat. If you don't or can't consume milk, choose lactose-free products or other foods that can provide sources of calcium, such as calcium-fortified orange juice, canned sardines, tempeh, or collard greens.

## Fruits

Fruits, indicated by the red band, are the next largest group represented on the pyramid. Any fruit or 100 percent fruit juice is included in the fruit group. Most fruits are a good source of vitamins A and C, as well as fiber and potassium. As with vegetables, it is best if you eat a variety of fruits in order to benefit from a wide range of vitamins. Canned fruits and fruit juices are not as nutritious as fresh fruits, mainly because sugar has been added to them.

A glass of orange juice has as much calcium as a glass of milk, which is great news if you happen to restrict the amount of dairy in your diet.

## Meat and Beans

Meat, poultry, fish, dry beans or peas, eggs, nuts, and seeds all fall into the meat and bean category, indicated by the purple band. Dry beans and peas are in this group and in the vegetable group. It's important to choose lean or low-fat meat and poultry sources, such as lean cuts of pork, ham, chicken, and turkey. Select fish rich in omega-3 fatty acids, like salmon and trout. Sunflower seeds and almonds are excellent sources of vitamin E. Avoid processed meat products like sausages, bacon, salami, and bologna, which are often loaded with salt and preservatives and are high in saturated fats.

## Oils

A sliver of the pyramid, the yellow band, represents oils, which are fats that are liquid at room temperature. MyPyramid recommends a daily allowance for oils (based on your age, gender, and activity level) that are high in monounsaturated and polyunsaturated fats, such as vegetable oils, nuts, and avocados. Solid fats, like butter, margarine, and shortening, should be counted in your daily discretionary calories (see below) because they contain saturated and trans fats, which raise the "bad" (LDL) cholesterol levels in the blood.

## Discretionary Calories

MyPyramid gives you a number of extra calories you can "spend" on solid fats and sugars each day. Or you might eat a higher-calorie version of a food you're craving. Or use these

Nuts have a bad reputation, but they are high in unsaturated fats, which are good for you. The body needs these fats to transport vitamins and build vital substances.

calories to eat more food from a food group than your personalized plan recommends. It's up to you, but beware, most discretionary allowances range from 100 to 400 calories a day, and those extra calories can add up quickly.

## Physical Activity

Eating your recommended servings from each food group is great, but it's not enough to maintain your health. Physical activity is just as important, as represented by the person walking up a flight of steps on the MyPyramid symbol. At a bare minimum,

Some people believe intense gym time can make up for a lack of daily exercise. However, there's no substitute for being physically active once a day, which can be as simple as playing Frisbee.

doing thirty minutes of moderate-intensity physical activity daily is recommended. But, ideally, children and teenagers should be physically active sixty minutes each day. If that sounds like it is too overwhelming for you to do each day, don't forget that riding your bike to school, tossing a Frisbee in the park with a friend, or taking ballet class counts toward that hour of exercise every day.

# Glossary

**calorie** A unit of measure that indicates how much energy a food will provide.

**carbohydrate** An essential structural part of living cells and a macronutrient that provides the human body with the energy it needs to function. Carbohydrates are found in grains, starches, fruits, and sugar.

**cholesterol** A substance found in animal tissues and some foods (such as red meat and eggs) that is used in building cell tissues and hormones. In humans, it can build up in the arteries, causing dangerous blockages.

**coronary heart disease** A condition in which blood flow to the heart is restricted by cholesterol buildup in the arteries.

**fiber** Coarse, indigestible plant matter that aids digestion and can help lower cholesterol.

**high-density lipoprotein (HDL)** A substance that transports cholesterol easily through the bloodstream and is associated with a decreased risk of coronary heart disease; often called "good" cholesterol.

**low-density lipoprotein (LDL)** A substance that transports cholesterol and is associated with a greater risk of coronary heart disease; often referred to as "bad" cholesterol.

**minerals** Inorganic substances found in nature and vital to the nutrition of plants, animals, and humans.

**nutrition** The processes by which an individual takes in and utilizes food material.

obese Excessively overweight, generally at least 20 percent more than one's ideal body weight.

protein A macronutrient found in meats, beans, nuts, and some other foods that is responsible for repairing and building cells in the body.

saturated fat A fat or fatty acid that has been linked to increased risk of coronary heart disease and is solid at room temperature.

trans fat An unhealthy substance that is made when food manufacturers turn liquid oils into solid fats by adding hydrogen (in a process called hydrogenation). Trans fat can be found in vegetable shortenings, some margarines, crackers, cookies, snack foods, and other foods made with or fried in partially hydrogenated oils.

unsaturated fat An oil or fatty acid that may reduce levels of LDL cholesterol.

vitamin Any of a group of organic substances essential to the nutrition of most animals and some plants. Vitamins are present in food and are sometimes produced in the body, but they do not provide energy.

American Dietetic Association (ADA)
120 South Riverside Plaza, Suite 2000
Chicago, IL 60606-6995
(800) 877-1600
Web site: http://www.eatright.org
   This is the nation's largest organization for nutritional
   professionals who promote healthy eating and lifestyle habits.
   Its Web site features nutrition information and recipes.

Bam! Body and Mind
Web site: http://www.bam.gov
   From the home page, click on "Food & Nutrition" at this
   site just for kids and teens by the Centers for Disease
   Control and Prevention.

Dietary Guidelines for Americans
Web site: http://www.healthierus.gov/dietaryguidelines/index.html
   Download the entire eighty-page *Dietary Guidelines for
   Americans 2005*.

Food and Nutrition Information Center (FNIC)
Agricultural Research Service, USDA
National Agricultural Library, Room 105
10301 Baltimore Avenue
Beltsville, MD 20705-2351
(301) 504-5719
Web site: http://www.nal.usda.gov/fnic

The FNIC staff is made up of nutrition professionals, most of whom are registered dieticians, who provide a wealth of knowledge about food and nutrition. The Web site contains more than 2,000 links to reliable nutrition information.

GirlsHealth.gov
Web site: http://www.girlshealth.gov
This site, developed by the Office on Women's Health in the U.S. Department of Health and Services, is for girls between the ages of ten and sixteen and covers a myriad of topics, including nutrition.

KidsHealth.org
Web site: http://www.kidshealth.org
Loads of information from the Nemours Foundation on all sorts of health and fitness topics for kids and teens, including a number of recipes.

Mayo Clinic
Web site: http://www.mayoclinic.com
Under "Healthy Living" on the home page, link to several articles about teen health and weight loss.

MyPyramid.gov
Web site: http://www.mypyramid.gov
Key in your age, gender, and activity level to find personalized food guidance based on the 2005 *Dietary Guidelines for Americans.*

National Institutes of Health (NIH)
Building 1
1 Center Drive
Bethesda, MD 20892

(301) 496-4000

Web site: http://www.nih.gov

NIH is the nation's medical research agency, part of the U.S. Department of Health and Human Services. NIH scientists investigate ways to prevent disease and improve the health of all Americans.

U.S. Department of Agriculture (USDA)

Food and Nutrition Service (FNS)

3101 Park Center Drive

Alexandria, VA 22302

(703) 305-2062

Web site: http://www.fns.usda.gov

The USDA and the U.S. Department of Health and Human Services jointly issue the *Dietary Guidelines for Americans* every five years. FNS provides children and adults of all ages with nutrition education materials on how to improve their diets and their lives.

U.S. Food and Drug Administration (FDA)

Center for Food Safety and Applied Nutrition

5600 Fishers Lane

Rockville, MD 20857

(888) INFO-FDA (463-6332)

Web site: http://vm.cfsan.fda.gov/label.html

The FDA is responsible for protecting the public health by assuring the safety, efficacy, and security of human and veterinary drugs, medical devices, cosmetics, and our nation's food supply.

## Web Sites

Due to the changing nature of Internet links, Rosen Publishing has developed an online list of Web sites related to the subject of this book. This site is updated regularly. Please use this link to access the list:

http://www.rosenlinks.com/faq/mypy

# For Further Reading

Bean, Anita. *Awesome Foods for Active Kids: The ABCs of Eating for Energy and Health.* Alameda, CA: Hunter House, 2006.

D'Elgin, Tershia. *What Should I Eat? A Complete Guide to the New Pyramid.* New York, NY: Ballantine Books, 2005.

Jukes, Mavis, and Lilian Wai-Yin Cheung. *Be Healthy! It's a Girl Thing: Food, Fitness, and Feeling Great.* New York, NY: Crown Books for Young Readers, 2003.

Schroeder, Barbara, and Carrie Wiatt. *The Diet for Teenagers Only.* New York, NY: Regan Books, 2005.

Shanley, Ellen, and Colleen Thompson. *Fueling the Teen Machine.* Palo Alto, CA: Bull Publishing, 2001.

Ward, Elizabeth M. *The Pocket Idiot's Guide to the New Food Pyramids.* New York, NY: Alpha, 2006.

"America's Eating Habits: Changes and Consequences."
    USDA.gov. 2000. Retrieved October 3, 2006 (http://www.
    ers.usda.gov/publications/aib750/aib750.pdf).

Bickerstaff, Linda. *Nutrition Sense* (The Library of Nutrition).
    New York, NY: The Rosen Publishing Group, Inc., 2005.

D'Elgin, Tershia. *What Should I Eat? A Complete Guide to
    the New Pyramid.* New York, NY: Balantine Books, 2005.

"Dietary Guidelines for Americans 2005." HealthierUS.gov.
    2005. Retrieved October 3, 2006 (http://www.healthierus.
    gov/dietaryguidelines/).

Faiella, Graham. *The Food Pyramid and Basic Nutrition:
    Assembling the Building Blocks of a Healthy Diet* (The
    Library of Nutrition). New York, NY: The Rosen
    Publishing Group, Inc., 2005.

"Inside the Pyramid." USDA.gov. 2005. Retrieved October
    3, 2006 (http://www.mypyramid.gov/pyramid/
    index.html).

McCarthy, Rose. *Food Labels* (The Library of Nutrition).
    New York, NY: Rosen Publishing Group, Inc., 2005.

"The Nutrition Source: Knowledge for Healthy Eating."
    Harvard School of Public Health. 2006. Retrieved
    October 3, 2006 (http://www.hsph.harvard.edu/
    nutritionsource/).

Schlosser, Eric. *Chew on This: Everything You Don't Want
    to Know About Fast Food.* Boston, MA: Houghton
    Mifflin, 2006.

Schlosser, Eric. *Fast Food Nation: The Dark Side of the All-American Meal.* New York, NY: HarperPerennial, 2002.

Shanley, Ellen, and Colleen Thompson. *Fueling the Teen Machine.* Palo Alto, CA: Bull Publishing Company, 2001.

Tecco, Betsy Dru. *Food for Fuel* (The Library of Nutrition). New York, NY: Rosen Publishing Group, Inc., 2005.

# Index

## Photo Credits

Designer: Evelyn Horovicz